The Emancipation Proclamation

TURNING POINTS IN U.S. HISTORY

The Emancipation Proclamation

Dennis Brindell Fradin

Marshall Cavendish Benchmark
New York

Dedication

For my granddaughter, Anna Rose Fradin, with love

Marshall Cavendish Benchmark
99 White Plains Road
Tarrytown, NY 10591
www.marshallcavendish.us

Text and maps copyright © 2008 by Marshall Cavendish Corporation
Maps by XNR Productions

All rights reserved. No part of this book may be reproduced or utilized in any form or by any means electronic or mechanical including photocopying, recording, or by any information storage and retrieval system, without permission from the copyright holders.

All Internet sites were available and accurate when sent to press.

Library of Congress Cataloging-in-Publication Data

Fradin, Dennis B.
The Emancipation Proclamation / Dennis Brindell Fradin.
p. cm. — (Turning points in U.S. history)
Includes bibliographical references and index.
ISBN-13: 978-0-7614-2038-5
1. United States. President (1861-1865 : Lincoln). Emancipation Proclamation—Juvenile literature. 2. Lincoln, Abraham, 1809-1865—Juvenile literature. 3. Slaves—Emancipation—United States—Juvenile literature. 4. Slavery—United States—History—Juvenile literature. 5. United States—Politics and government—1861-1865—Juvenile literature. I. Title. II. Series.
E453.F73 2007
973.7'14—dc22
2006025345

Photo research by Connie Gardner

Cover: *Emancipation Proclamation* painting by A.A. Lamb
Title Page: An 1865 lithograph
Page 28: © 2007 Michael Escoffery/Artists Rights Society (ARS), New York

Cover Photo: Francis G. Mayer/CORBIS
Title Page: The Granger Collection
The photographs in this book are used by the permission and through the courtesy of: *Getty Images:* Hulton Archives/Stringer, 6; Time and Life Pictures, 38; *The Granger Collection*: 8, 12, 20, 21, 22, 30, 32, 34, 36; *Corbis*: Bettmann, 14, 26, 27, 31; *North Wind Picture Archives*: 10, 18; *Art Resource*: Michael Escoffery, 28. Time Line: Bettmann/CORBIS, 42-43.

Editor: Deborah Grahame
Publisher: Michelle Bisson
Art Director: Anahid Hamparian

Printed in Malaysia
1 3 5 6 4 2

Contents

CHAPTER ONE:	Slavery in the Thirteen Colonies	7
CHAPTER TWO:	"All Men Are Created Equal"	11
CHAPTER THREE:	Slavery Divides the Nation	15
CHAPTER FOUR:	President Lincoln Faces a Crisis	19
CHAPTER FIVE:	President Lincoln's Decision	23
CHAPTER SIX:	"The Great Act of the Age"	29
CHAPTER SEVEN:	An End and a Beginning	35
	Glossary	40
	Timeline	42
	Further Information	44
	Bibliography	46
	Index	47

This painting shows the Jamestown settlers building a fort and houses with thatched roofs.

CHAPTER ONE

Slavery in the Thirteen Colonies

England settled Virginia, its first American **colony**, in 1607. Twelve years later, in 1619, about twenty black people arrived at Jamestown, Virginia. **Slavery** had begun in England's American colonies.

England eventually founded, or took over, twelve other American colonies besides Virginia: Massachusetts, New Hampshire, New York, Connecticut, Maryland, Rhode Island, Delaware, Pennsylvania, North Carolina, New Jersey, South Carolina, and Georgia. More than 100,000 slaves lived in the thirteen colonies by the time England's last colony, Georgia, was begun in 1733. The number of slaves had soared to 326,000 by 1760.

THE EMANCIPATION PROCLAMATION

A tobacco label from the early 1700s shows a Virginia plantation owner relaxing while his slaves work.

SLAVERY IN THE THIRTEEN COLONIES

The original thirteen North American colonies were settled between 1607 and 1733.

All thirteen colonies allowed slavery. However, the vast **majority** of slaves lived in the Southern colonies, where they worked in the tobacco and rice fields. By 1776 about nine-tenths of the 530,000 slaves in the colonies lived in the South.

Colonists cheered as the Declaration of Independence was read in Philadelphia in 1776.

CHAPTER TWO

"All Men Are Created Equal"

On July 4, 1776, American leaders issued the Declaration of **Independence**. This document announced that the thirteen colonies were now the United States of America.

The Declaration of Independence stated, "We hold these truths to be **self-evident**, that all men are created equal." Many Americans hoped that the declaration would **outlaw** slavery. For how could the new country talk about equality when more than half a million of its people were slaves? However, slavery was still allowed in all thirteen of the new states. American leaders decided not to **condemn** slavery in the declaration.

THE EMANCIPATION PROCLAMATION

Framers of the United States Constitution met in Philadelphia at the Constitutional Convention in 1787. George Washington is shown presiding.

Eleven years later, in 1787, American leaders gathered to create the new country's **Constitution**. Slavery was a topic of argument among the framers of the U.S. Constitution. By 1787 many Northerners had turned against slavery. Some of the convention's Northern **delegates** argued that the constitution should end slavery.

In the South, however, slavery was growing. Southern delegates threatened that they would have nothing to do with a Constitution that banned slavery.

The Northerners backed down. As a result, the U.S. Constitution, like the Declaration of Independence, did nothing to condemn slavery.

The invention of the cotton gin made the South a top cotton producer. It also increased the demand for slaves to grow and pick the cotton.

CHAPTER THREE

Slavery Divides the Nation

Meanwhile, state governments in the North had begun to outlaw slavery. Massachusetts became the first state to outlaw slavery in 1780. Other Northern states followed. By the mid-1800s slavery was gone in the North.

On the other hand, the number of slaves in the South continued to grow. This was especially true after 1793, when the invention of the cotton gin made cotton a big moneymaking crop. By 1840, 2.5 million people in the Southern states were black slaves. In fact, African-American slaves comprised one-seventh of the nation's **population**.

THE EMANCIPATION PROCLAMATION

Slave and Free States in 1860

The Underground Railroad

The Underground Railroad was a secret network of houses and other hiding places where escaped slaves stayed on their flight northward. People who hid slaves in their homes were called stationmasters. Thomas Garrett, a stationmaster in Delaware, helped about 2,500 slaves. Levi and Katie Coffin, stationmasters in Indiana and Ohio, sheltered more than 3,100 runaway slaves.

People who led slaves northward were called conductors. After escaping from slavery herself, Harriet Tubman became a famous Underground Railroad conductor. She led more than three hundred other slaves out of bondage.

The arguing over slavery became more heated in the early and mid-1800s. Hundreds of Northern **abolitionists** helped slaves to escape along the Underground Railroad. The abolitionists also spoke of fighting a war to end slavery.

White Southerners spoke of states' rights. They believed each state had the right to decide for itself about such important matters as slavery. They also threatened to fight a war to protect those rights.

Thousands witnessed Lincoln's inauguration in March 1861. The U.S. Capitol was still under construction.

CHAPTER FOUR

President Lincoln Faces a Crisis

The 1860 presidential election was one of the most important in the nation's history. Whoever was elected would have a lot to say about the future of slavery—and of the country.

Abraham Lincoln of Illinois won the election. People close to him believed he was determined to end slavery. In 1858 Lincoln had said, "I believe this government cannot **endure**, permanently half slave and half free."

Southerners strongly disagreed with Lincoln's stand on slavery. Southern states began to **secede** from the United States even before Lincoln took office. South Carolina went first. It seceded on

THE EMANCIPATION PROCLAMATION

This 1861 cartoon humorously predicts the fate of states that seceded from the Union.

December 20, 1860. Eventually eleven Southern states seceded. They joined together as the **Confederate States of America**, a separate country. It was called the Confederacy or the South for short. The Confederates organized a powerful army. They elected their own president, Jefferson Davis of Mississippi.

PRESIDENT LINCOLN FACES A CRISIS

Charleston residents witnessed the bombardment at Fort Sumter, the first battle of the Civil War.

President Lincoln and people in the North were determined to put the divided country back together and to end slavery. The United States—also called the Union, or simply the North—prepared for war with the Confederates.

On April 12, 1861, Confederates fired on a Union fort at Charleston, South Carolina. This marked the start of the Civil War. The four-year conflict would cost more American lives than any other war in the country's history.

President Abraham Lincoln (1809–1865), photographed in 1862.

CHAPTER FIVE

President Lincoln's Decision

By early 1862 President Lincoln was giving serious thought to freeing the slaves. Many abolitionists were urging him to do so. After all, they pointed out, was the war not being fought largely over slavery?

President Lincoln agreed. The time had come to act against slavery. Lincoln had a problem, though. Four states—Delaware, Maryland, Kentucky, and Missouri—allowed slavery, but remained loyal to the Union. Many white residents of these states would be angry if Lincoln freed their slaves. The four states might even join the Confederate side.

By the spring of 1862 President Lincoln had made his decision. He would free *some* of the slaves. He decided to write a paper explaining how this would work.

Famous Abolitionists

There were many notable Americans among the nation's thousands of abolitionists. Former slave Frederick Douglass founded the *North Star*, an antislavery newspaper. Newspaper publisher William Lloyd Garrison once publicly burned a copy of the Constitution because it permitted slavery. Abolitionist lawmakers included Pennsylvania congressman Thaddeus Stevens, who called slavery "a curse, a shame, and a crime." Massachusetts Senator Charles Sumner was once attacked and nearly killed in the U.S. Senate chamber because of his opposition to slavery. Other Americans who worked to end slavery include author Lydia Maria Child, founder of the country's first children's magazine; black abolitionist and teacher Charlotte Forten; and minister Theodore Parker.

Back in the 1860s the fastest way to send messages was by telegraph. Nearly every day, President Lincoln walked a short way from the White House to the telegraph office in the War Department building. There he read the latest news on the war and relaxed by chatting with the telegraph operators.

One day in June 1862, Lincoln told Major Thomas Eckert, head of the War Department's telegraph staff, that he wanted to write something. Eckert provided paper, and Lincoln began writing in the telegraph office. For a few weeks, the president worked on his document during his telegraph office visits. When he finished, Lincoln told Major Eckert that he had written a paper that would result in "freedom to the slaves in the South."

On July 22, 1862, President Lincoln met with his cabinet, or group of advisers. He read the paper he had written to the cabinet members. On the first day of the coming year, the document explained, President Lincoln was going to declare that all slaves in Confederate-held territory were free.

The Telegraph

The telegraph was invented by Samuel F. B. Morse and others in 1837. It was the first mechanical device to send messages through electricity. Morse also developed Morse code, a system of dots and dashes used to represent letters in telegraph messages.

THE EMANCIPATION PROCLAMATION

Lincoln listened as his cabinet discussed the paper. Secretary of State William H. Seward had a suggestion. Seward pointed out that the Union was doing poorly on the battlefield. Lincoln should not issue the document until the outlook for winning the war improved. Otherwise, his plan for freeing the slaves in the Confederacy might seem like empty words.

Lincoln and members of his cabinet discussed ways to implement, or set into motion, the document that would declare all slaves free.

PRESIDENT LINCOLN'S DECISION

Dead Confederate soldiers on the battlefield of Antietam, or Sharpsburg.

President Lincoln decided to follow Seward's advice. However, over the next few weeks the situation grew worse for the Union. For a while it appeared that the Confederates might capture Washington, D.C., the U.S. capital.

The tide began to turn on September 17, 1862. That day the Battle of Antietam was fought in Maryland. Each side lost about 13,000 men. Antietam was the war's bloodiest day of fighting. The Confederates were forced to retreat, so the battle was widely viewed as a Union victory.

Five days later, on September 22, 1862, President Lincoln issued his document about slavery. It declared that on New Year's Day of 1863, slaves in lands under Confederate control were to be proclaimed "forever free." This document became known as the Preliminary Emancipation Proclamation.

This painting depicts a dramatic scene in which slaves learn that they are to be emancipated.

CHAPTER SIX

"The Great Act of the Age"

People had two questions during the one hundred days leading up to January 1, 1863. First, why would slaves in Maryland, Delaware, Kentucky, and Missouri not be included in the **proclamation**? These were areas the Union controlled. Second, since the proclamation would target areas the Union did not control, how would it free even a single slave?

The answer to the first question was that Lincoln did not want the four states to join the Confederacy. The slaves themselves would provide the answer to the second question. Southern slaves overheard their owners talking about Lincoln's **emancipation** plan. Word spread from

THE EMANCIPATION PROCLAMATION

cabin to cabin and from plantation to plantation: on the first day of the new year, they would be free.

Meanwhile, during those one hundred days, Lincoln wrote the Emancipation Proclamation. This was the paper that would actually declare the Confederate slaves free. Up to the last moment he crossed out words, rewrote sentences, and pasted together paragraphs.

Finally, on the afternoon of January 1, President Lincoln prepared to sign the final copy with a few friends looking on in the White House. "I never felt more certain that I was doing right than I do in signing this

The final page of the Emancipation Proclamation.

paper," Lincoln remarked. Then he signed the Emancipation Proclamation.

The document was a turning point in American history. Knowing that President Lincoln had declared them free, thousands of Southern slaves ran away to Union military camps and Northern cities. Slaveholders could do little about this because so many white Southern men were away fighting in the Confederate army. Thousands of other slaves were freed as Union forces conquered Confederate territory and put the proclamation into effect.

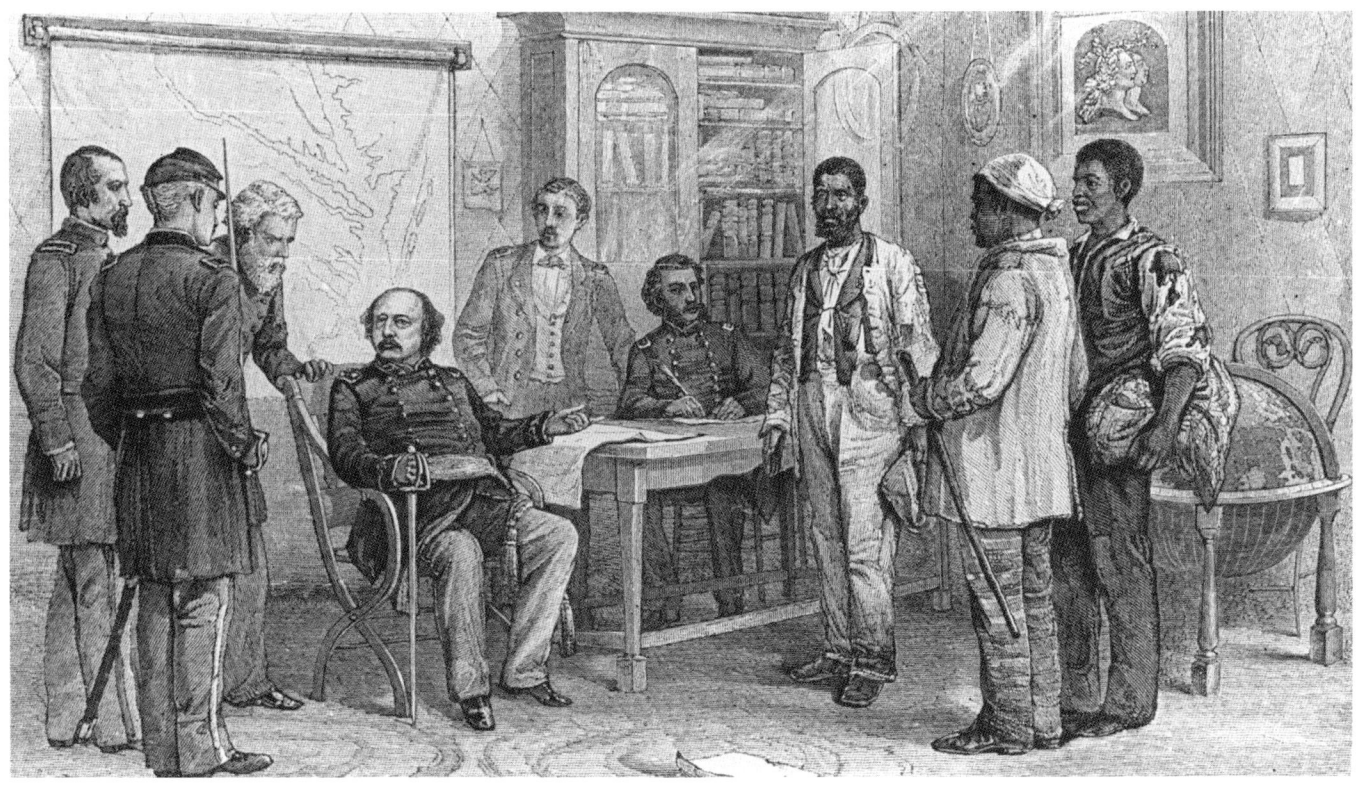

Union soldiers interview runaway slaves. Black men were welcome to enlist in Union forces, and they fought bravely.

THE EMANCIPATION PROCLAMATION

The Emancipation Proclamation also declared that the former slaves would be "received into the armed service of the United States." Many newly freed men joined the Union army and navy. In all, 200,000 African Americans served in Union forces. Since they were fighting for their own freedom, as well as for the Union, the 200,000 black troops served heroically. In fact, they were a major reason why the Union won the Civil War.

A studio portrait of a black Union soldier taken during the Civil War.

As Lincoln had hoped, Kentucky, Missouri, Maryland, and Delaware remained loyal to the Union. Yet, even in places where the proclamation did not declare them free, many slaves seized their own liberty by running away.

Vice President Hannibal Hamlin considered Lincoln's emancipation of the slaves "the great act of the age." Lincoln himself was proud of his proclamation. He called it "the central act of my administration, and the great event of the nineteenth century."

The black people who had been freed expressed what the Emancipation Proclamation meant to them. They called 1863—when the proclamation was announced—the Year of **Jubilee.**

An 1863 engraving shows freed slaves crossing into Union-held territory.

CHAPTER SEVEN

An End and a Beginning

Thanks largely to the Emancipation Proclamation, most of the nation's four million slaves were freed during the Civil War. They continued to run away and to be liberated by Union troops. Thousands were freed when state governments outlawed slavery. Yet, when the Union won the war in the spring of 1865, there were still many slaves awaiting freedom.

The U.S. government finished the job of ending slavery. Toward the end of the war, Congress passed the Thirteenth Amendment to

THE EMANCIPATION PROCLAMATION

Celebrating Freedom

To this day, African Americans celebrate the end of slavery. On January 1 some churches hold services honoring the anniversary of the Emancipation Proclamation. Celebrations are also held on September 22, the anniversary of the Preliminary Emancipation Proclamation. People in some places honor the anniversary of the date their ancestors were freed. For example, thousands of slaves in Texas were not freed until June 19, 1865. This was the origin of Juneteenth, a holiday held by African Americans in Texas on June 19. Juneteenth has grown and is now celebrated in many communities around the country. Some people honor February 1 as National Freedom Day. On that date in 1865, President Lincoln signed the Thirteenth Amendment. The amendment freed all remaining American slaves later that year.

A U.S. postage stamp commemorating the seventy-fifth anniversary of the Thirteenth Amendment.

the Constitution. It went into effect on December 6, 1865. "Neither slavery nor involuntary servitude . . . shall exist within the United States," the Thirteenth Amendment declared. It ended slavery in the United States forever.

Freedom was the first step in a larger struggle for African Americans. The former slaves soon discovered that freedom did not mean equality. Long after the Year of Jubilee, black Americans suffered **discrimination** in housing, education, and employment. They were deprived of their voting rights. Thousands of them were murdered by white mobs, especially in the South.

Slavery Continues

Many people are shocked to learn that slavery still exists. The United Nations estimates that 100 million children and many millions of adults live as slaves or in slave-like conditions, mainly in South America, Asia, and Africa. Modern-day slavery is sometimes due to debt bondage, a practice in which families who owe rich people money must work until the debt is paid. Often the debt is so large that it can never be repaid. Generation after generation, the debtors must work on the wealthy people's farms or in their factories or mines.

THE EMANCIPATION PROCLAMATION

Dr. Martin Luther King Jr. addressed demonstrators at the March on Washington in August 1963.

A famous civil-rights protest was held during the one-hundredth anniversary year of the Emancipation Proclamation. In August 1963 more than 200,000 people gathered in the nation's capital for the March on Washington. They demanded equality for all Americans. Dr. Martin Luther King Jr. made his great "I have a dream" speech at this demonstration. It is a dream that many people still have, nearly 150 years after President Lincoln issued the Emancipation Proclamation.

Glossary

abolitionists—People who are determined to end slavery.

colony—A settlement built by a country outside of its borders.

condemn—To declare wrong or evil.

Confederate States of America (or Confederacy)—The country composed of eleven Southern states that seceded from the Union in the nineteenth century.

Constitution—A framework of government.

delegates—People who act on behalf of other people.

discrimination—Unfair treatment or bias, often based on race, religion, or gender.

emancipation—Freedom; the act of freeing.

endure—To last.

GLOSSARY

independence—Freedom or self-government.

jubilee—A time of great joy.

majority—A number greater than half of the total.

outlaw—To disallow or deny; forbid.

population—The number of people in a particular place.

proclamation—An announcement.

secede—To leave or withdraw.

self-evident—Clear without needing proof; obvious.

slavery—The practice of owning people against their will.

Timeline

1607—Jamestown, Virginia, becomes the first permanent English settlement in what will be the United States

1619—Slavery begins in England's American colonies with the arrival of about twenty black people at Jamestown

1733—England establishes Georgia, its thirteenth and final American colony

1776—The thirteen colonies issue the Declaration of Independence, announcing that they have become the United States

1780—Massachusetts becomes the first state to outlaw slavery

1793—The cotton gin is invented

mid-1800s—Slavery has been ended in the North, but it is flourishing in the South

1860—Abraham Lincoln of Illinois is elected president of the United States; the Southern states begin seceding

1607   *1776*   *1860*

1861—April 12: The Civil War between the Confederacy and the Union begins

1862—September 22: President Lincoln issues the Preliminary Emancipation Proclamation

1863—January 1: President Lincoln issues the Emancipation Proclamation, which eventually leads to the end of slavery in the United States

1865—February 1: President Lincoln signs the Thirteenth Amendment

April 9: The Union wins the Civil War

April 15: President Lincoln dies after being shot by John Wilkes Booth

December 6: The Thirteenth Amendment goes into effect and frees any remaining slaves

1963—The March on Washington is held in Washington, D.C., during the one-hundredth anniversary year of the Emancipation Proclamation

2013—150th anniversary of the Emancipation Proclamation

1863   1865   1963

Further Information

BOOKS

Altman, Linda Jacobs. *Slavery and Abolition in American History*. Berkeley Heights, NJ: Enslow, 1999.

Burchard, Peter. *Lincoln and Slavery*. New York: Atheneum, 1999.

Holford, David M. *Lincoln and the Emancipation Proclamation in American History*. Berkeley Heights, NJ: Enslow, 2002.

Roberts, Russell. *Lincoln and the Abolition of Slavery*. San Diego: Lucent, 2000.

Tackach, James. *The Abolition of American Slavery*. San Diego: Lucent, 2002.

FURTHER INFORMATION

WEB SITES

For an introduction to the Emancipation Proclamation
usinfo.state.gov/usa/infousa/facts/democrac/24.htm

National Archives Online Exhibits Web site, with a link to material about the Emancipation Proclamation
www.archives.gov/exhibits/

For information about the creation of the Emancipation Proclamation
memory.loc.gov/ammem/alhtml/almintr.html

Bibliography

Contemporary Forms of Slavery (pamphlet). Geneva, Switzerland: Centre for Human Rights, United Nations Office at Geneva, 1991.

Franklin, John Hope. *The Emancipation Proclamation*. Garden City, NY: Doubleday, 1963.

Guelzo, Allen C. *Lincoln's Emancipation Proclamation: The End of Slavery in America*. New York: Simon & Schuster, 2004.

Miers, Earl Schenck. *The Emancipation Proclamation*. New York: Grosset & Dunlap, 1969.

Ploski, Harry A., and Roscoe C. Brown Jr., eds. *The Negro Almanac*. New York: Bellwether, 1967.

Wiggins, William H. Jr. *O Freedom!: Afro-American Emancipation Celebrations*. Knoxville: University of Tennessee Press, 1987.

Index

Page numbers in **boldface** are illustrations.

maps
    Original Thirteen Colonies, 9
    Slave and Free States in 1860, 16

abolitionists, 17, 23, 24
African Americans, **31**, 31–33, **32**,
    34, 36–39, **38**. *See also* slavery
Antietam, Battle of, 27, **27**

civil rights movement, **38**, 39
Civil War, 17, 21, **21**, 23, 26–27, **27**,
    32
Confederacy, 20, 31
Constitution, **12**, 13, 24
    Thirteenth Amendment, 35–37
cotton, **14**, 15

Davis, Jefferson, 20
debt bondage, 37
Declaration of Independence, **10**,
    11
discrimination, 37
Douglass, Frederick, 24

Emancipation Proclamation
    anniversary of, 33, 36, **36**, 37, 39
    Preliminary, 23–25
    significance, 31–33
    timing, 25–27, **26**, 33
    writing, 24–25, **30**, 30–31

Fort Sumter, 21, **21**

Garrison, William Lloyd, 24

holidays, 36

Jubilee, Year of, 33, 37
Juneteenth, 36

King, Martin Luther, **38**, 39

Lincoln, Abraham, **18**, 19, 21, **22**,
    23–33, **26**

North, **11**, 13, 21, 31
    slavery in, 15, 23–26, **26**, 29

population data, 7, 9, 15

secession, 19–20, **20**
Seward, William H., 26
Sharpsburg, Battle of, 27, **27**
slavery
    in the United States, 7–13, **8**, **14**
        ending, 23–37, **28**, **31**, **34**
        in the Union, 23–26, **26**, 29, 33
    outside the United States, 37
South, 9, 11, 13, **14**, 15, 17, 19–20,
    20, 31, 37. *See also* Texas;
    Virginia

states' rights, 17

telegraph, 24, 25
Texas, 36
thirteen colonies, 7–13, **9**, **10**, **12**
Tubman, Harriet, 17

Underground Railroad, 17
Union, 21, **31**, 32
    slavery in, 23–26, **26**, 29, 33

Virginia, **6**, 7, **8**, 9

About the Author

Dennis Fradin is the author of 150 books, some of them written with his wife, Judith Bloom Fradin. Their recent book for Clarion, *The Power of One: Daisy Bates and the Little Rock Nine*, was named a Golden Kite Honor Book. Another of Dennis's recent books is *Let It Begin Here! Lexington and Concord: First Battles of the American Revolution*, published by Walker. The Fradins are currently writing a biography of social worker and antiwar activist Jane Addams for Clarion and a nonfiction book about a slave escape for National Geographic Children's Books. Turning Points in U.S. History is Dennis Fradin's first series for Marshall Cavendish Benchmark. The Fradins have three grown children and three young grandchildren.